Norton Young Readers

An Imprint of W. W. Norton & Company

Independent Publishers Since 1923

DOING BUSINESS

Shawn Harris

Whose business is this?

The baby does business in a diaper.

This is not baby business.

Daddy does business
in the bathroom.

This is not
daddy business.

Who did this?

This is no place

for business.

Her business is too big.

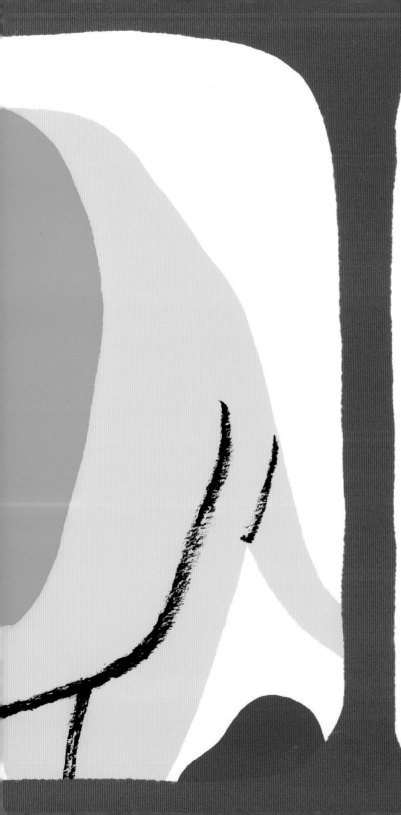

His business

is too small.

Is it bird business?

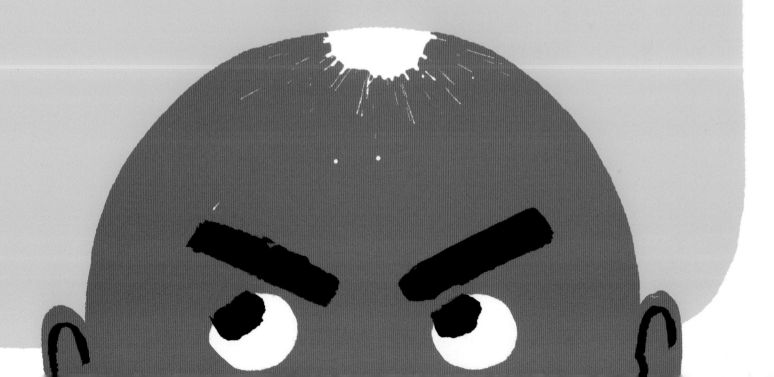

No sir.

Is it funny business?

Is it stinky business?

For sure.

Wait—
Who did
this business?

You did this business?

This is good.

Good business.

Cats do business

in a box.

Fish do business

in the
water.

Everyone
is doing
business.

Business is good.

But not this.

This is bad business.

Who did this?

The DOG
did this!

This is *NOT*

where dogs do business.

Dogs do business

OUTSIDE!

Good business.

For Mom and Dad,
for teaching me good business.

The illustrations are ink and brush with digital color.

Copyright © 2021 by Shawn Harris

All rights reserved
Printed in China
First Edition

For information about permission to reproduce selections from this book, write to
Permissions, W. W. Norton & Company, Inc., 500 Fifth Avenue, New York, NY 10110

For information about special discounts for bulk purchases, please contact
W. W. Norton Special Sales at specialsales@wwnorton.com or 800-233-4830

Manufacturing by Toppan Leefung Printing, Ltd.
Book design by Shawn Harris and Semadar Megged

ISBN 978-1-324-01566-6

W. W. Norton & Company, Inc., 500 Fifth Avenue, New York, N.Y. 10110
www.wwnorton.com

W. W. Norton & Company Ltd., 15 Carlisle Street, London W1D 3BS

2 4 6 8 0 9 7 5 3 1